NEWFIE TO THE RESCUE!

A Lifeguard Dog Story

by Meish Goldish

illustrated by Tom Connell

New York, New York

Credits

Cover photo, © Grisha Bruev/Shutterstock.

Publisher: Kenn Goin
Editor: Jessica Rudolph
Creative Director: Spencer Brinker

Library of Congress Cataloging-in-Publication Data

Names: Goldish, Meish, author.
Title: Newfie to the Rescue! A Lifeguard Dog Story / by Meish Goldish.
Description: New York, New York : Bearport Publishing, [2017] I Series: Hound
    Town Chronicles I Summary: At Hound Town Lake, Emma meets the newest
    lifeguard, a Newfoundland, and learns how the dog's webbed feet and
    rudder-like tail are used to save struggling swimmers.
Identifiers: LCCN 2016042382 (print) I LCCN 2016053540 (ebook) I ISBN
    9781684020171 (library) I ISBN 9781684020683 (Ebook)
Subjects: I CYAC: Rescue dogs—Fiction. I Newfoundland dog—Fiction. I
    Dogs—Fiction. I Lifeguards—Fiction.
Classification: LCC PZ7.G56777 Li 2017 (print) I LCC PZ7.G56777 (ebook) I DDC
    [E]—dc23
LC record available at https://lccn.loc.gov/2016042382

For more information, write to Bearport Publishing Company, Inc., 45 West 21st Street,
Suite 3B, New York, New York 10010. Printed in the United States of America.

10 9 8 7 6 5 4 3 2 1

CONTENTS

WELCOME TO

HOUND TOWN

A Doggone Nice Place to Live!

Population:
25,000 people
20,000 dogs

CHAPTER 1

Life at the Lake

Splash! Emma Preston leaped off a **pier** and dove into the cool waters of Hound Town Lake. Emma was a strong swimmer—stronger than most nine-year-olds. Her father had taught her how to swim when she was only five. She loved coming to the town lake with her family every summer.

Emma tilted upward and glided to the lake's surface. Her head popped out of the water, and she bobbed up and down. She could see her parents near the beach. Her father was giving a swimming lesson to her five-year-old brother, Hunter.

Emma swam over to her family. Dad held Hunter and placed him gently on his stomach in the water. Hunter closed his eyes tight. Emma could tell he was nervous.

"Relax, Hunter," Emma said. "Dad won't let go of you. Loosen your arms and legs a little." Hunter let his arms and legs dangle.

"That's it!" cried Emma. "Now, start paddling." Hunter kicked his arms and legs wildly, splashing water on everyone.

"Whoa!" Emma laughed. "Not so hard."

Dad smiled at Emma. "Thanks, sweetie," he said. "Do you remember when I gave *you* swimming lessons?"

"Yeah," Emma said. Then she turned to her brother. "Hunter, Dad's a great teacher. Do what he says and you'll become a super swimmer—like me."

"Okay!" Hunter smiled.

Emma asked her parents, "Mom, Dad, is it okay if I walk along the beach for a while?"

Her parents nodded. "But be back for lunch in about thirty minutes," said Mom.

Emma marched out of the water. The warm sand felt good between her toes. It was a hot July day, but a slight breeze whipped through Emma's hair.

As she strolled down the beach, Emma gazed at all the people who had come to enjoy the day. Many had their dogs with them.

One boy stood on the pier and threw a tennis ball over the water. His Labrador retriever ran down the pier and flew after the ball. The

HOUND TOWN'S
JULY 4TH BLAST

dog caught the tennis ball mid-air and landed—*PLUNK*—right into the lake! Emma was amazed at the dog's leaping abilities.

Then Emma spotted a white, shaggy haired dog walk out of the lake and stop near a man sleeping on a towel. The dog shook its body from head to tail, spraying water and sand all over the man! Emma quietly giggled to herself.

In a part of the lake that was off limits to swimmers, a group of people were working on boats and a floating **platform**. The workers were preparing for tomorrow night's Fourth of July fireworks show. That was one event Emma and her family never missed!

Walking farther down the beach, something caught Emma's eye—two big, green chairs. A man wearing a T-shirt that said "LIFEGUARD" sat in the taller chair. In the shorter chair was . . . a giant dog!

The man and dog were focused on the swimmers in the water. Emma was curious, so she walked over to them. "Uh, hi!" she called in a loud voice.

The man glanced down at her and smiled. "Hello! Is everything all right?" he asked.

"Yes," Emma said. "I'm just wondering why you have a dog with you."

"I'm Roger," the man said. "This is my dog, Newfie. He's a Newfoundland. He's also a lifeguard, like me."

Emma looked surprised. "A dog who's a lifeguard?" She chuckled. "You're joking, right?"

"It's true," Roger replied as he patted the dog's head. "Newfie's trained to rescue people who are **stranded** in boats or struggling in the water."

Emma wondered—*How could a dog save a person in the water?* She wanted to ask more questions, but she knew she shouldn't bother a lifeguard who was on **duty**. Besides, it was almost lunchtime, and she needed to get back to her family.

"Well, it was nice meeting you," she said. "I'm Emma Preston. See you later. Bye, Newfie."

"See you, Emma," said Roger.

Newfie looked calmly at Emma and started panting with his tongue hanging out of his mouth. Emma thought, *Wait until Mom, Dad, and Hunter hear about this!*

CHAPTER 2

Cool Treats

That night at dinner, Emma told her family about Newfie. "It's really cool that a dog can be a lifeguard!" she exclaimed. "I wonder how he's trained."

"Why don't you ask Roger the next time you see him?" Mom suggested.

Then, Dad asked, "So, who wants to go out for some ice cream?"

"We do!" Emma and Hunter cried together.

The family climbed into their car and drove to Dogs 'n' Cones, a popular ice cream shop in Hound Town. The store sold ice cream for its human customers and freshly baked doggy treats for **canines**.

Emma looked over the menu. All the ice cream flavors had funny names. "I'm going to get a Bark Berry Crunch cone."

Hunter said, "I'm going to get Lemon Twister. That's yummy."

The family chose a table outside the shop and began to eat their ice cream. It was a nice, cool treat for a warm July evening.

Crunch! Crunch! A fluffy Pomeranian sitting beneath the next table was munching on a doggy treat while its owner read a newspaper.

Suddenly, Emma heard a bark behind her. She turned around and—surprise! It was Roger and Newfie.

"Mom, Dad, this is Roger, the lifeguard," Emma said. "And this is his dog, Newfie."

Roger shook hands with Emma's parents. "And who's this little guy?" he asked, looking at Hunter.

"This is my brother, Hunter," Emma said proudly. "He's five. He's learning how to swim."

Newfie walked over to Emma and lapped her face with his wet tongue. "Aw, Newfie! Doggie kisses!" she laughed.

Then, Newfie **plodded** toward Hunter. "Newfie's as tall as I am!" The boy smiled and looked wide-eyed at the giant dog. The canine licked Hunter's face and the boy giggled.

"You two can pet him," Roger said. "As you can see, Newfie's very friendly." Both Hunter and Emma petted and nuzzled the Newfoundland. They liked the feel of his thick, soft fur.

Suddenly, the dog put his paw on Hunter's hand and took a big lick of the boy's ice cream. "I guess Newfie really likes Lemon Twister!" Hunter squealed. "He's so goofy! Goofy Newfie!"

Emma looked at Roger. "At the beach, Newfie was so calm. Now he's so silly."

"That's because this morning Newfie was on lifeguard duty," Roger explained. "When he's working, he must stay focused on his job. But when he's off-duty, he can be his playful, goofy self!"

Mom glanced down at Emma. "Didn't you have a question you wanted to ask Roger?" she said.

"Oh, yeah!" Emma said to Roger. "How do you train a dog to be a lifeguard?"

"Good question," Roger replied. "I'll tell you what. Tomorrow morning, Newfie and I will be at the lake early. We'll be practicing lifesaving exercises before the beach opens to the public. If you like, your family can watch how I train Newfie."

Mom and Dad nodded their heads. "We'll be there," Emma said with excitement. "Thank you!"

CHAPTER 3

The Workout

Early the next morning, the Prestons ate breakfast and then drove to Hound Town Lake. Roger and Newfie were already on the beach.

"Good morning," Roger said. "Newfie and I are about to start our workout."

Roger pointed to the red vest on Newfie's back. "This is Newfie's **harness**. He wears it when he's on duty," Roger explained. "If someone in the water is struggling, the person can grab a hold of it."

"Or Newfie can swim to the person with a **lifeline** like this." Roger held up a round tube with a long rope attached to it. "Watch. I'll swim into the lake and pretend to be a swimmer who's in trouble."

Roger dropped the lifeline on the beach and swam out about fifty feet from shore. Then he called, "Newfie! Help! Bring me the lifeline!"

Newfie immediately picked up the long rope with his mouth and began to swim out into the lake. The Prestons watched in astonishment.

"Wow!" Hunter cried.

When Newfie reached Roger, the lifeguard grabbed the lifeline. The dog kept the rope in his mouth and turned around. Then he pulled Roger back to shore.

"Good job, Newfie!" Roger said, **praising** and petting the dog.

The Prestons clapped their hands. "Newfie is so fast!" Emma cried.

"Yes," Roger said as he used a towel to dry off. "I'll show you how he's able to do it."

The Prestons leaned in close to the dog. Roger held up one of Newfie's paws. "You see this extra skin between his toes?" Roger asked.

"Oh, it kind of looks like a duck's foot," Emma said.

"Exactly," Roger replied. "Newfoundland dogs have **webbing** 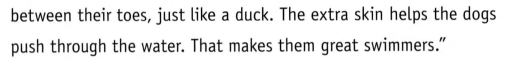 between their toes, just like a duck. The extra skin helps the dogs push through the water. That makes them great swimmers."

"Cool!" said Hunter.

Roger pointed to the dog's long tail. "Can you guess how his tail helps him swim?"

Hunter and Emma stared at Newfie's long, furry tail. "Hmmm," said Hunter.

"Does it work like a fish's tail?" asked Emma.

"It's very similar, Emma," replied Roger. "Newfie uses his tail to help him control the direction he's swimming in."

"A duck and a fish!" Hunter exclaimed.

"And, get this. Newfoundlands are very strong. They're even strong enough to pull a boat with up to twenty people inside!" Roger said.

"Can you believe that, Emma?" said Dad.

"No way! Not possible!" cried Emma.

Roger smiled. "Want to see?" he said.

There was a large green rowboat on the beach. Roger pulled it to the edge of the water. "Okay, Prestons," he said. "Everybody on board."

Mom, Dad, Emma, and Hunter climbed in. Roger pulled on a rope attached to the front of the boat, bringing it onto the lake.

"I'll row us out onto the lake," Roger said. Then he looked at Newfie, who was still standing on the beach. Roger **commanded**, "Newfie, stay."

"Of course, we don't add up to twenty people," Roger told the family. "But this will still show you how strong Newfie is."

When the boat was far enough out, Roger stopped rowing. He called to shore, "Newfie! Help! Rescue us!"

The family watched Newfie rush into the water and swim straight toward the boat. After reaching the rowboat, the dog grabbed the rope attached to the front of it and held it with his mouth. Then he turned around and began to swim toward the beach with **determination**. At first, the boat moved slowly.

"Holy cow!" Emma cried. "He's actually pulling us!"

"Yay!" Hunter clapped.

Soon, the boat picked up speed and they reached the shore in no time. When Newfie got to the beach, he shook the water off his fur, then patiently sat down. The Prestons hopped out of the boat and thanked Roger. They gave Newfie lots of pats and hugs.

"Great job, Newfie!" Emma cried.

"You're so strong!" Hunter added. Newfie seemed to love the attention.

A crowd of people began to gather, waiting for the beach to open. "It's time for us to go on duty," Roger said. "July Fourth is always a busy day here. Will I see you tonight at the fireworks show?"

"Oh, yes!" Emma said as the family waved good-bye.

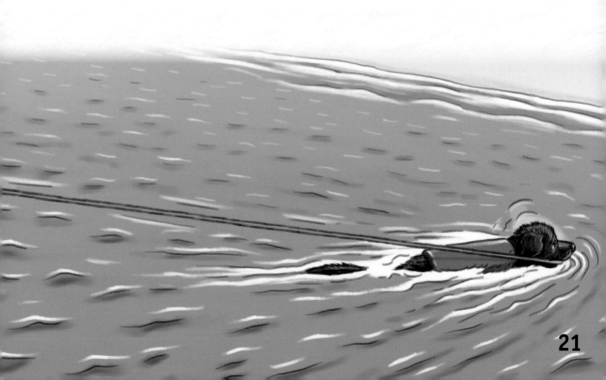

CHAPTER 4

A Night of Lights

That evening, the Prestons returned to Hound Town Lake. The lake was calm and peaceful. Nobody was in the water swimming, but hundreds of people were gathered on the beach to watch the fireworks show. Many brought their dogs.

The family **scouted** the area, looking for a good place to view the fireworks. After picking a spot, Emma saw Roger and Newfie nearby and called to them. "Would you watch the fireworks with us?" she asked.

Roger and Newfie came over, and Emma scratched the dog behind his ears. "Happy Fourth of July, Newfie!" Emma said. "I think you're going to love the fireworks tonight!"

Out on the lake, workers on the fireworks platform checked that everything was ready. Then a voice was heard over a loudspeaker: "Ladies and gentlemen, please rise for our **national anthem**." The crowd sang the anthem together. The Prestons laughed when Newfie began to howl near the end of the song.

It was a perfect night for a fireworks display. A cool breeze blew across the lake. Emma and Hunter could hardly wait for the dazzling colors to appear in the sky.

BOOM! The show began. First, dozens of red, white, and blue

stars sparkled in the sky over the lake. Then, several rockets soared upward. They left bright trails of silver and gold as they climbed higher and higher. With each new set of lights that exploded across the sky, the crowd cheered and applauded. Everyone's eyes were glued to the colorful show overhead.

••• 🦴 •••

However, on the crowded beach, Hunter wasn't able to see the show clearly. The tall grown-ups standing in front of him were blocking his view. The little boy **craned** his neck. Then he stood on his tiptoes to get a better look, but that didn't help. The beach was just too packed with people. Hunter was frustrated that he was missing the fireworks.

While his family continued to gaze at the sky, Hunter quietly wandered away. Farther down the beach, he saw a rowboat on the sand, at the edge of the water. Hunter walked up to the boat and slowly climbed in. He stood on the walls of the rowboat at the front end, where the two sides joined together. Now he could see the fireworks above the crowd!

Just then, the boat began to slide into the water. Frightened, Hunter struggled to keep his balance as the boat bobbed and drifted away.

Suddenly, a wave **jolted** the rowboat. Hunter lost his balance and fell into the lake! He tried to grab the side of the boat, but his hands slid off the slippery wall.

As he splashed in the water, Hunter took a gulp of water. The boy panicked and screamed into the night air, "Help! Help!" Unfortunately, no one on the beach could hear him. The fireworks drowned out the sound of his voice.

CHAPTER 5

To the Rescue!

Emma continued to watch the fireworks show with her parents and Roger and Newfie. With every new explosion in the sky, she joined the crowd with shouts of *Ooooh!* and *Ahhh!*

Suddenly, Newfie's head perked up and he began to bark loudly. *Woof! Woof!* Then the dog sniffed the air.

Emma glanced around and realized that Hunter was gone. "Where's Hunter?" Emma cried. Her parents and Roger looked around desperately. "Hunter!" Mom screamed. "Where are you?"

Just then, Newfie **bolted** down the beach. Roger and the Prestons ran behind him, trying to keep up. Finally, Newfie moved closer to the water, ran into the lake, and started swimming.

"Oh no, could Hunter be in the lake?" Dad asked.

"It's possible," Roger replied. "But if Hunter's there, Newfie will find him. He can pick up a person's scent even in the water."

Meanwhile, Hunter struggled to stay above the surface of the lake. He paddled hard with his arms and legs, splashing water all around him. Soon, Hunter spotted Newfie swimming nearby. "Newfie!" Hunter **spluttered**. "Help!"

The dog swam right up to the little boy. Hunter saw that Newfie had no harness—and no lifeline either! Instead, Hunter grabbed on to the dog's collar. Then Newfie turned back toward the shore, pulling the boy with him.

On the beach, Mom, Dad, Emma, and Roger looked nervously at the inky black waters of the lake. Roger took out his flashlight and shined it on the lake. First, the light revealed the empty rowboat floating in the water. Then the light showed two figures in the water approaching the beach—Newfie and Hunter!

"There they are!" Roger cried. "Newfie's pulling Hunter to shore. And Hunter is kicking with his legs. That's a very good sign. It means he's awake and **conscious**."

As Newfie and Hunter got closer to the beach, Roger ran into the lake. Then he picked Hunter up, carried him to the sand, and sat him down.

"Are you all right, Hunter?" Dad asked.

"Yes," Hunter said proudly. "I stayed above the water!"

Mom gave Hunter a serious look. "Hunter, you should have never walked away from us. Why did you do that?" Hunter explained that he wanted to find a better spot to watch the fireworks.

"Don't ever do that again," his father said in a stern voice. "You could have drowned."

"I'm sorry," said Hunter. Then he looked at his sister. "Emma, yesterday you told me to paddle with my arms and legs. That's what I did. I paddled, and it worked. I swam!"

Emma hugged her brother. "There's someone else you should thank," she said, pointing to Newfie. The big dog was busy shaking water off his fur. Hunter got up and walked over to him and got sprayed with water.

Hunter laughed and gave Newfie a big hug. "Newfie," Hunter said, "you're the best lifeguard dog ever. I want to be a great swimmer, just like Emma . . . and just like you!" Newfie licked Hunter's face.

Newfie to the Rescue!
A Lifeguard Dog Story

1. How does Emma show that she cares about her brother, Hunter?

2. Pick a word that best describes Newfie when he is at work. Then pick another word that best describes the dog when he is not working. Give examples of things Newfie does in the story that made you choose those words.

3. What is happening in this scene?

4. How was Newfie able to find Hunter when the boy was struggling in the lake?

5. Do you think a dog lifeguard is as capable as a human lifeguard? Give reasons for your answer.

bolted (BOHLT-id) moved rapidly

canines (KAY-nyenz) dogs

commanded (kuh-MAN-did) gave an order to an animal to do something

conscious (KAHN-shuss) being awake, alert, and able to think

craned (KRAYND) stretched out in order to see something

determination (dih-tur-mih-NAY-shuhn) a strong will to accomplish something

duty (DOO-tee) the work required by one's job

harness (HAR-niss) a device attached to an animal that allows a person to hold onto the animal

jolted (JOHLT-id) moved suddenly or jerkily

lifeline (LIFE-line) a special rope used to rescue someone who is drowning

national anthem (NASH-uh-nuhl AN-thuhm) the official song of a country

pier (PEER) a structure built over water, used as a walkway or a landing place for boats

platform (PLAT-form) a flat, raised structure where people can stand

plodded (PLAHD-id) walked heavily or slowly

praising (PRAYZ-ing) giving enthusiastic words of approval

scouted (SKOUT-id) searched for something

spluttered (SPLUT-urd) made a noise as if spitting

stranded (STRAN-did) left helpless in a strange or dangerous place

webbing (WEB-ing) skin between the toes that helps with swimming

About the Author

Meish Goldish is an award-winning author of more than 300 books for children. His book *City Firefighters* won a Teachers' Choice Award in 2015. He especially enjoys writing fiction, nonfiction, and poetry about animals. Growing up in Tulsa, Oklahoma, Meish liked to play with the many dogs in his neighborhood. Now a resident of Brooklyn, New York, he continues to frolic among the friendly canines there.

About the Illustrator

Tom Connell has been a professional illustrator since 1987. He works in many styles, but his specialty is realism. Originally painting in gouache and acrylics, he moved on to airbrush and now draws most of his work digitally. He has created artworks for many advertising campaigns, magazines, and several hundred children's books. He lives with his family and two border collies close to the River Kennet in Reading, England.